dada

mama

This book belongs to:

maisie

....

me

teddy

In loving memory of my granduncle, Dr. Joseph T. Narh, who greatly influenced my life and that of so many people in my extended family.
Samuel

For my wonderful parents, with love and gratitude.
Jo

First published in the United Kingdom in 2019 by Lantana Publishing Ltd., London.
www.lantanapublishing.com | info@lantanapublishing.com

American edition published in 2019 by Lantana Publishing Ltd., UK.
Second impression 2019.

Text © Samuel Narh 2019
Illustration © Jo Loring-Fisher 2019

The moral rights of the author and illustrator have been asserted.

Distributed in the United States and Canada by Lerner Publishing Group, Inc.
241 First Avenue North, Minneapolis, MN 55401 U.S.A.
For reading levels and more information, look for this title at www.lernerbooks.com
Cataloging-in-Publication Data Available.

Printed and bound in Europe.
Original artwork using mixed media, finished digitally.

ISBN: 978-1-911373-57-5
eBook ISBN: 978-1-911373-60-5

Maisie's Scrapbook

Samuel Narh   Jo Loring-Fisher

LANTANA PUBLISHING

Maisie rubs petals between her fingers.
Tears roll down her cheeks.
Mama won't let her play with the bull by the fence.

She's the little girl in Dada's tall tales.

Mama says tomato.
Dada says aamo.
They hug her in the same way.
She's as relentless as spring rain.

Maisie hides behind the shrubs.
Mama looks for her behind the trees.
A flock of birds cheers them on.

Dada points out turtles swinging on chandeliers of stars in the night sky.

Mama wears linen.
Dada wears kente cloth.
They praise her in the same way.
She's as bright as a summer's day.

Maisie hurls leaves into the air.
She wants them to stay on the trees.
The bull frightens her into Mama's arms.

Dada shows her clouds painting
pictures of ancient worlds in the sky.

Mama cooks risotto.

Dada cooks jollof rice.

They nag her in the same way.

She's as spirited as autumn leaves.

A smile runs across Maisie's face.
She sits in Mama's rocking chair.

She bucks and pulls the horns
of a bull made of wood.

She's the hero in Dada's tall tales.

Mama plays viola.
Dada plays marimba.
They love her in the same way.
She's as pure as winter's snow.